SHIMMEREE

Written By:
STEPHEN COSGROVE

Illustrated By:
ROBIN JAMES

A Serendipity Book

Dedicated to Dian and Mo Morris.
They have shared with me
more than I can repay.

Stephen

In a mirror of sunrise glitter, dawn was born again in a land of crystalline splendor. As the sunshine crept across the diamond mountains, it shimmered from the crystal trees and flowers that made up this wondrous land.

For, you see, all living things in this land were cast from either glass, diamond or crystal. The only colors were splashes of blue, silver and gold.

In this magic land, many strange crystal creatures frolicked in the dancing lights of day. There were crystal-like birds called glimmerings, smiling little lizards called beamers and, most beautiful of all, horse-like creatures called lightasoars, who had wings made of delicate diamonds so they could fly wherever the eye could see.

The youngest of all the lightasoars was called Shimmeree. She was very small, like a precious stone, and as curious as a cat. She would spend all of her days chasing after rainbows or trying to catch the sun.

Everything would have stayed all sparkle and glitter in this magic place had not Shimmeree, as she was flying about one day, discovered a small pile of dust caught in the corner of a crystal rock. Well, not only had she never seen dust before, but the color of it was most amazing. This dust wasn't crystal blue or silver but rather a greyish-brown.

She studied it from side to side and then rushed off to tell her fellow creatures what she had found.

At first the other creatures didn't believe the little lightasoar, the mere thought of something new was just impossible. Finally, they decided to humor her and reluctantly followed her to the crystal rock.

Sure enough, just as Shimmeree had told them, there was that pile of dust. None of them had ever seen anything like it before, Just as they prepared to sweep it away, the dust settled and there nestled on the rock was a pearl-shaped seed.

Well, the creatures didn't like this one little bit. Not only was there a pile of dust, which was unheard-of, but also a seed, the likes of which they had never seen before.

"We can't have this!" said the leader of the lightasoars.

"It must be destroyed!"

"Oh yes!" cried the glimmerings and the beamers.

"Destroy the seed before it harms us."

Shimmeree stood there for a moment and then stomped her feet angrily. "No!" she said. "Why should we destroy it just because we don't know what it is?"

"Oh, Shimmeree," the leader patiently. "Look at it. It's not blue, silver or gold. It's not even crystal."

"Please, please!" cried Shimmeree. "Let me take care of the seed. If something starts to happen, you can destroy it."

The leader thought for a moment and finally agreed. After all, with Shimmeree watching nothing bad could happen.

True to her word, Shimmeree stayed near the dust and the pearl-shaped seed day in and day out. Then, one day the seed crackled, creaked and groaned. As she watched in amazement, a small shoot, ever so slowly, reached out to the sun. Most amazing of all was its color, the likes of which she had never seen . . . the color green.

With a flip of her tail and a twitch of her ears, Shimmeree flew into the air and rushed to find the other creatures. After she told them what she had seen, they all rushed fearfully back to the rock.

"I knew we should have destroyed it!" cried the beamers. "Look at it!" shuddered the glimmerings. "You can't see through it like crystal. It just has to be evil."

The leader of the lightasoars looked around and then shouted in alarm, "Oh, no! We're all catching its color!" Sure enough, the small green plant had been reflected over and over again in the crystal formations. Everything had turned a distinct shade of green.

The creatures all stomped and snorted and would have destroyed the plant if Shimmeree had not come up with a daring plan.

"Look!" she cried. "The sun is setting. We can't destroy this thing in the dark. Who knows what terrible fate would befall us if we couldn't see what we were doing?"

"She's right," said the frightened leader of the lightasoars. "We'll come back at the first light of day and destroy this thing."

The other creatures were just as frightened as he and quickly agreed. So, they hurried off to safely sleep the night away.

When she was sure that everyone was fast asleep, Shimmeree quietly flew back to the crystal rock and the little green shoot.

By the soft reflections of starlight, she carefully scooped up the pile of dust and flew to the highest peak of the diamond mountain.

It was there that she safely hid the tiny bit of dust and the ever growing plant. Knowing that it would be safe, she contentedly flew back to where the other creatures were sleeping.

At the first crack of dawn all the creatures marched to where the little pile of dust had been, much to their surprise it was gone!

"Maybe it blew away in the night?" mused Shimmeree innocently.

"Who cares?" asked the other creatures. "We're just glad that it's gone forever."

It was at that exact moment that the little plant began to bud and blossom, flooding the diamond mountain and the sparkling sky with the most beautiful red hue.

"Oh no!" they cried. "We are doomed!" "No," laughed Shimmeree, "come with me and I'll show you that there is nothing to fear."

The creatures, although very frightened, followed her to the top of the mountain.

Nervously, they approached the spot where Shimmeree had flown the night before. And there, even to her surprise, instead of the small green plant stood the most beautiful red rose.

As the creatures looked on in wonder, the sun began to rise in all its splendor, and colors of all sorts spread throughout the land.

"See?" said Shimmeree gleefully. "You had nothing to fear but fear itself."

So, from that day forward, color was brought into the land of crystalline things, and all the creatures learned not to fear that which they didn't understand.

SO, IF AMONG YOUR TRAVELS YOU
FIND A THING UNKNOWN, THINK
OF CRYSTAL SHIMMEREE AND
THE SEED THAT SHE WAS SHOWN.